For Mum, who loves cats,
and for Dad, who is allergic—A.S.

Library of Congress Cataloging-in-Publication Data is available.

ISBN 978-0-545-57604-8

10 9 8 7 6 5 4 3 2 1   14 15 16 17

Printed in China   53

First American edition, June 2014

Naughty Kitty!

by Adam Stower

Orchard Books • New York
An Imprint of Scholastic Inc.

Lily wanted a doggy,
but her mom said dogs were too messy,
too smelly, and far too much trouble.
So she got Lily something else . . .

He was a bit scruffy . . .
and no good at tricks . . .

but otherwise he
was quite cute,

especially when you
tickled his tummy.

And Mom was right,

he wasn't any trouble at all . . .

at first.

But then, just for a moment,

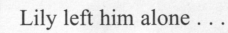

Lily left him alone . . .

It was a catastrophe.

What a mess!

Lily couldn't understand it.

How could you?
Eight fish sticks, all the cookies,
plums, pickles, Mom's pink party cake,
Dad's pork chop, the orange pop, two teaspoons,
and a dirty sponge!

And she'd just fed him
a whole bowl of Kittibix!

Lily told Kitty to sit still

until she'd finished tidying the kitchen.

There was to be no messing, no mischief,

and absolutely no scratching.

Lily was getting cross.

Surely Kitty couldn't cause any more trouble?

But by dinnertime things had gone from bad to worse.

and I still don't know how
you stole all my sausages!

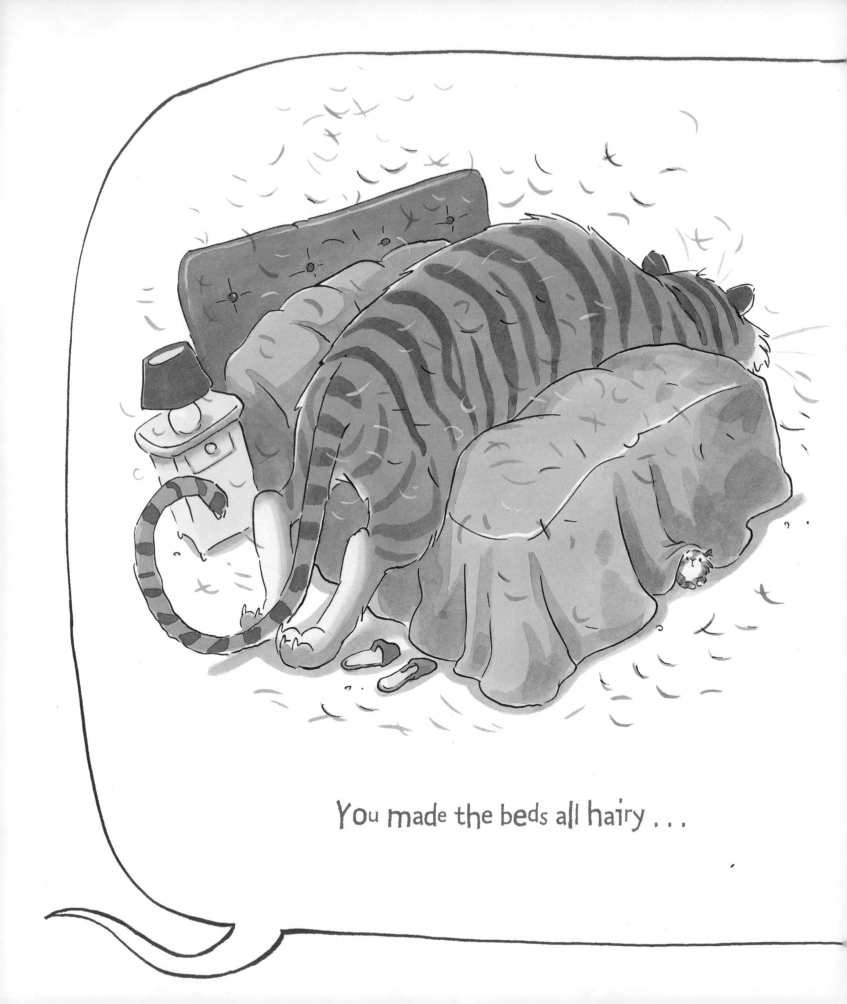

You made the beds all hairy . . .

and as for Mom's rug –
I can't even talk about that.
It was REVOLTING!

But just then they heard a long, low

GRRRROOOWWWWWWL!

There was something in the garden.

Something with teeth . . .

something with claws . . .

something with STRIPES!

It was Pat, the dog from next door.

Lily yelled!

Kitty YOWLED . . .

. . . and the bad dog ran away.

Perhaps Kitty wasn't so naughty after all.

In fact, Lily decided he was completely fantastic
and he deserved a whole box of Kittibix,
a tummy rub, and a quiet, cozy snuggle on the sofa.

So that's just what they did.

AMAZING and TRUE!

FLUFFBUN'S RETURN

Doris Battenburg, 72, of 10 Wye Avenue, Sea Knit, was overjoyed by the recent return of her long lost cat, Fluffbun. "He followed Pat, my dog, home at dinnertime yesterday. eyes aren't what they used to but I'm pretty sure it's him. 's grown quite a bit since t time I saw him . . . but at's not surprising, it was 30 years ago."

Doris with Pat and Fluffbun.

MONKEY BUSINESS

It looks like hungry thieves have been targeting poor Mr. B. Nana's fruit

Re Que especi of a BIC in place a